LEVEL **2** READER

My Magical Friends

Mermaid Song

by Amy Edgar

illustrated by Jomike Tejido

SCHOLASTIC INC.

For my magical daughters, Sophia and Fuji
—J.T.

ISBN 978-1-338-30266-0

10 9 8 7 6 5 4 3 2   19 20 21 22 23

Printed in Jiaxing, China   68
First printing 2019

Book design by Joan Moloney

Shelby and Isabella were best friends.

Isabella knocked on Shelby's front door.

Shelby opened the door.

"Hi! Come on back to my room," said Shelby.

Shelby was playing with her toy castle.
She loved to imagine as she played with the tiny
houses, the castle, and the enchanted forest.
"It's warm and sunny today," said Isabella.
"Let's take the play set outside."
"Great idea," said Shelby.

"But first, let's put on our crowns," said Shelby.
"After you, Princess Shelby," said Isabella, giggling.
"And here is yours, Princess Isabella," said Shelby,
giggling even more. They looked like real
princesses.

Shelby and Isabella set up the play set next to a small pond in Shelby's backyard.

"It's fun to play with this outside," said Isabella.

"Yes," agreed Shelby, "but do you know what could be even more fun?"

Isabella was not sure.

Shelby pulled a small gold box out of her pocket. She opened it.

"The magic bracelet!" said Isabella.

Shelby's grandma had given her the bracelet. It had magical powers. Last time Shelby put it on, the two friends traveled to an enchanted forest with a castle!

Isabella helped Shelby put on the bracelet.
It glowed for a second.
They grabbed hands and looked down at the
bracelet. They felt a funny tug and a tingle.
They saw a flash of light.

The girls blinked and looked around.
They were not in Shelby's backyard anymore!
A castle stood nearby. And they were standing
on a beach.

"The magic bracelet worked again!" shouted
Isabella.

"Amazing!" whispered Shelby.

Both girls took off their shoes and walked
into the water.

"Did you hear something?" asked Shelby.

"It sounds like someone singing a sad song," said Isabella.

"I think it's coming from over by that big rock," said Shelby.

"Let's go!" said Isabella.

As they got closer, the sound got louder.

Then they saw something truly magical.
It was a mermaid. She was beautiful.
The mermaid cried as she splashed the
water with her shimmery tail.

"Hello," said the girls.

"Oh, hello, princesses," said the mermaid.

"My name is Pearl."

"Do you understand what she is saying?" asked Isabella.

"I do," said Shelby. "It is because I am wearing the magical bracelet."

"She thinks we are princesses," Shelby told
Isabella. "And her name is Pearl."
"I may not understand her words, but I can tell
she is sad," said Isabella.
"Pearl," asked Shelby, "why are you so sad?"
"A seagull has taken my lucky shell," said Pearl.
A tear rolled down the mermaid's cheek.

"We would like to help you," said Shelby.
"That is so kind of you!" said Pearl. She wiped
away her tears.
"Do you know where the seagull went with
your shell?" asked Shelby.

"The seagull flew away and dropped it on that beach," said Pearl.

Shelby told Isabella everything that Pearl had said.

"Oh no!" said Isabella. "And Pearl can't get the shell because she can't walk on the sand and has to stay in the water!"

"Let's get that shell back for her!" said Shelby.

"Yes," said Isabella, "let's go!"

"How will we know which shell is yours?" Shelby asked Pearl.

"My shell has a golden heart on it," said Pearl. "And when you hold it up to your ear, you can hear a mermaid singing."

"We will do our best to find it," said Shelby. "Let's go, Isabella."

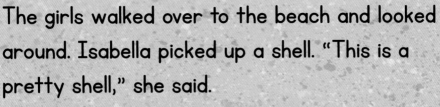

The girls walked over to the beach and looked around. Isabella picked up a shell. "This is a pretty shell," she said.

"It is," said Shelby. "But that shell does not have a golden heart on it."

"That sounds like a really special shell," said Isabella. "We have to find it!"

Then they spotted a seagull. They ran toward it.
It flew away.

"That could be the mean, old seagull that took
Pearl's shell," said Shelby.

"Hey, look at this shell!" called Shelby. She gently picked it up.
"It has a golden heart! This must be the one!" said Isabella.

Shelby and Isabella put their heads close together
and listened to the shell.
"I hear something!" said Isabella.

"It sounds like ocean waves," she added.

"Like a mermaid song," said Shelby.

"I can't wait to show Pearl!" said Isabella.

The girls hurried back toward Pearl, who was waving to them from her rock.

"You did it, princesses!" said Pearl, smiling.
"You found my lucky shell!"
"It is a beautiful shell," said Isabella.
"We are so happy we could help you," said Shelby.
"I would like to thank you by singing a song,"
said Pearl.

"She wants to sing for us," said Shelby.
Pearl began to sing to the girls. It was happier
than the song she sang when they first met.
Shelby and Isabella thought it was the most
beautiful song they had ever heard.

"Thank you for the song, Pearl," said the girls.
"Thank you both for finding my lucky shell!" said
Pearl. "I want to give you each a shell to keep."
She handed them each a tiny seashell.
"Next time you visit a beach, look for the prettiest
shell," added Pearl. "You will know a mermaid is
close and think of me."
"We will," promised the girls.

With a flip of her shimmery tail, Pearl was back
in the water.

She waved at Shelby and Isabella before she
went under the waves.

Isabella sighed. "We met a real mermaid today,"
she said.

"And made her happy again," added Shelby.

It had been a wonderful day. But it was time
to go home. Shelby and Isabella held hands again
and looked down at the magic bracelet.

The bracelet glowed. It sparkled.
They felt a funny tug and a tingle.
They saw a flash of light.

Just like that, they were back in Shelby's backyard.
The play set was in front of them.
Shelby looked at her bracelet again.
A pretty seashell charm hung from it.

Shelby smiled at this new surprise and thought
of Pearl. She showed the charm to Isabella.
Then Isabella felt something in her pocket.
It was the tiny shell. They were holding gifts
from a mermaid!

"Wow! What a day!" said Isabella.
"What a magical day!" said Shelby.